AF438461

The Foot Fetish Café

And Other Tales of Fetishism and Erotic Humiliation

By Gray Fisher

Table of Contents

The Long Walk Home

Just 10 miles, Richard Landon thought. *I got this.* The night couldn't get any shittier, after all. His car wouldn't start AND his cell phone had died during the evening of business schmoozing. But he considered himself a fit guy, and despite the fact he was wearing dress shoes, the weather was good and he was sober enough, so making it home in time to relieve his wife with the kids so she could meet her friends for a girls' night out wouldn't be too much of a problem.

He'd have to keep a good pace though. She'd be very annoyed if he was more than just a little late, and didn't brook excuses well. When she'd learned of his thing for the feet of their former babysitter, she'd reacted…well, "poorly" would be an understatement. He still blanched at the memory of being tied to the bed, a sweaty moccasin strapped over his face, and left alone to contemplate his sin. Alone, that is, until Amber, the very sitter he lusted for, showed up during her college break to "babysit" for him while Becky and her friend Stephanie went out for the evening. Amber and her own friend Lauren – the one who had shared the incriminating photo of him worshipping Amber's feet in the car that fateful night – were cruel to him during those long hours tied down. Richard was certain she gave Becky the complete play-by-play of their relentless teasing the next day.

The dynamic of their marriage had shifted dramatically since, his wife taking every opportunity to lord his transgression and weakness for female feet over him. His wife could be quite the bitch, and he tried hard to not incur her wrath.

Although deep down, he had to admit to himself that her belittling and punishments were exciting to him. She could berate him with the best of them, and her creativity, in both words and deeds, could be astonishing. Often, in the end, he would climax, but it was small consolation as she always orchestrated things in such a way that his head would spin in embarrassment, to the point that he now shuddered to recall the abasement he'd suffered in exchange. At the peak of her ministrations – or in the case of Amber, her ministrations by proxy – there was certainly pleasure, but searing shame inevitably followed. She knew how to turn the screw.

So he walked briskly, the light breeze at his back, his mind occupied with the people he'd spoken with earlier. Some business connections, a few people he knew and some he'd met for the first time. And the women! Dressed to impress at a holiday season function. For a guy who loved legs and feet, that was one of the great bonuses of attending such events. Lots of short dresses and heels. The appetizer buffet just couldn't compete.

He'd just crossed 4th Ave. and felt like he was making some headway when a car pulled off into the shoulder just ahead of him. When he caught up, he peeked into the window as one does when trying to identify someone they ought to know, and was rewarded with the sight of a pretty brown-haired woman with tasteful makeup and a pleasant face, accented by high arching, and recently tweezed, eyebrows.

"Hi," he said. It was the first thing that popped into his head. "Do you need any help?"

"No, I'm good," she replied. "It just kind of looks like you do. I saw you at the party. Everything okay?"

"Not really. Car broke down. Walking home."

"Why not call an Uber?"

It was a logical question, and he was embarrassed to answer. "Um, phone battery's dead."

"Hah! Yeah, not your night, huh?" She flashed a smile full of exaggerated sympathy. "Well, I can summon one for you."

"You're a life saver, um…"

"Candace. I'm Candace Bloom."

"Thank you, Candace Bloom. I'm Richard Landon. Now that I think of it, I recall seeing you there too." Yes, he did indeed recall. Tall, with a brown leather miniskirt, sheer dark tan hose, and dark burgundy, open-toe heels with criss-crossing straps revealing much nylon on the top of her foot. She was engaged throughout the party by multiple men, and he had noticed her from afar. Sadly, he hadn't had the chance, or maybe the nerve, to approach her. "You're very kind."

"You know what, forget the Uber. I'm happy to give you a lift. Get in."

"Hey, um, thanks. It's only about eight or nine miles up the highway, then another off the exit. Very nice of you."

"No problem, not really out of the way," Candace said as Richard climbed in the passenger side of the blue Toyota SUV. "Just let me know where to exit."

As he strapped in, his eyes were at once draw to the tan nylon, shimmering in the light of the lamp post above. He fumbled for his seatbelt buckle. Upon hearing the click, Candace pulled out, and Richard noticed how fetching that shoe looked as it pumped the accelerator pedal. In a quarter mile, she took the ramp to Route 77. Her passenger continued to be transfixed as she gave the Toyota more gas.

"Do you attend these a lot?" Candace asked.

"Um, yeah, I try to make a couple a month. I find them pretty valuable." The words came out relaxed as he glanced up at the side of her pretty face, but they contradicted the feelings swirling inside of him.

The highway lights were creating something of a strobe effect on Candace's lower limbs. Her hose had a natural sheen to them to begin with, but the white beams effectuated "trails" of shimmer that were almost hypnotic as they played across her leg, right to left, right to left. His attention was helplessly drawn too to her right strappy sandal, skillfully going from the gas pedal to the brake. He heard her say something about making good connections, but really just enjoying being out around people after working at home most of the time. This group was new to her, she added.

Richard gave a polite "uh huh" and muttered that socializing in person had become a lost art. *Lost on me, for sure,* he added to himself. *I couldn't even gin up the courage to talk to this beautiful woman when we were in a crowded room.*

She glanced at him, flashing a winning smile. Richard wasn't sure whether or not she caught his eyes cast downward. When she returned her attention to the road ahead, he once again felt like he had license to gape, and now noticed her leather skirt had ridden up quite a bit, the slit on the right thigh widening with her movement. Was it intentional, he wondered, or just a natural result of her stop and go motions driving the car?

He felt a bead of sweat form on the right of his forehead, despite the cool air. Her right hand, beautifully manicured with red polished nails and decked out with several silvery rings, ran up and down her lower thigh, as if she was scratching an itch. It was magnetic. A hint of a dark brown welt peeked out each time her hand moved upward.

Richard could feel the blood rushing into his manhood, but it was not a concern since he was seated, in a mostly dark car, wearing fairly loose-fitting trousers. Candace's right hand took the wheel, and he returned his lustful gaze to the pump squishing down on the gas pedal. Miles passed behind them, and Richard didn't want this trip to end.

At about this time he noticed the aroma in the vehicle. A flowery perfume, mixed with a slight leathery scent from her skirt and maybe her heels. It was intoxicating. He inhaled deeply, then heard her speak again.

"Like the view?" Candace asked, a smirk on her lovely face.

"Um, I'm sorry?"

"I'm gonna go out on a limb and say you like limbs, especially female ones." She chuckled.

"Oh, uh, I just appreciate the ride, more than you know. Very nice of you."

"Oh, I think I know." She smiled at him, and he felt his cock grow another inch inside his pants.

The sound of the tires on the asphalt below and the rhythmic thumping of the highway grew louder in his ears, as the lamp posts continued the strobe effect on what he now knew were stockings, not pantyhose. She again became focused on the road. Busted, but embarrassingly unable to turn his gaze elsewhere, he continued looking toward the gas pedal, although he tried to be more subtle this time.

Candace made some more small talk, and he replied in kind. But every minute or so her right hand would come to rest on that luscious thigh, or play at the top of her stocking. Her tastefully long nails contrasted nicely with the nylon. He was coming undone. Where before, he hoped this lift would go on forever, now he couldn't wait for it to end before he made even more of an idiot of himself. He glanced at his watch. His wife was expecting him in 15 minutes, and Richard was confident he'd be home in plenty of time so as not to get an earful, or worse.

His breathing became deeper as he soaked in the show this woman seemed to be putting on for his benefit. Oh, that strappy shoe looked wonderful as it depressed the car's pedal. What delightful things she could do to him with that heel, with a fraction of the pressure she applied to the gas. Or even better, if she pressed more firmly than she was doing with the pedal.

He gazed longingly at her fingernails, following them up her leg, and for the first time saw a garter clasp. How he'd like to pleasure her with his head framed by that ensemble of nylon and probably silk. A woman like this no doubt wouldn't think of wearing cotton panties, or a pedestrian suspender belt. His stomach knotted at the thought, at the same time as his penis again stirred.

He then really noticed her partially bent right knee for the first time, the nylon stretched so taut over it so that he could just about make out the stocking's weave, even in the sporadic light. That little hint of a shadow every woman's joint exhibited seemed to be accentuated by the lamp posts, or the moonlight. He couldn't help but think of that bit of heaven on the backside of that knee, the sensation of sliding back and forth against the fabric that encased it. Unconsciously, he licked his lips.

"Don't forget to let me know where to exit," Candace said, interrupting his silent reverie.

"Oh, yes." He sharply looked out the window. While the scenery whizzing past was somewhat familiar, his stomach clenched at the realization that they had passed the exit to Braddock Ave. Indeed, he could tell they were well past it.

"Shit!"

"What is it, honey?"

"We missed it…um, I'm going to be late. Maybe you wouldn't mind turning around." His voice came out more panicked than he'd intended. His anxiety was spurred by the potential retribution from Becky if she had to miss more than a few minutes with her girlfriends from work.

Candace sighed. "Now that's going to be way out of the way, Richard. My boyfriend's cooking dinner and I need to get there before everything gets cold. He doesn't cook very often, and if I'm late he probably won't again anytime soon. At the very least, he'll insist I let him do things to me after dinner that I don't usually let him do."

Richard sucked in a breath at the statement. "But…it would just be a few minutes by car. It's only six or seven miles back…"

"I'm sorry, by the time I got up to the next exit to turn around, then dropped you…I'm afraid I can't." Her voice sounded sincere, but as she spoke she was blatantly stroking her upper leg, her eyes still on the road. "I'm sure there's an Uber nearby."

With that, she pulled onto the shoulder and slowed to a stop. "Good luck, Richard. It was very nice meeting you."

Dejectedly, taking one last look at Candace's hosed legs, he got out of the car and closed the door behind him. She pulled the Toyota away, and only at that moment did either of them remember that his phone battery was dead.

Richard turned north, and now walking into the wind, pulled the collar high up over his neck and began the long trek home. It'd take him almost two hours, he figured, essentially putting the kibosh on his wife's plans. Becky wouldn't be happy, not happy at all.

The Foot Fetish Café

These international trips stink, thought Lester Hoyt somewhere over the Atlantic. Initially, he'd found the prospect of traveling overseas in his position somewhat glamorous. Little did he know he'd be visiting mostly "emerging markets" – corporate speak for underdeveloped or former Soviet bloc countries that were looking to upgrade their infrastructure or become more active in the world economy.

His only consolation four hours into the 12-hour flight to the Ukraine was he was seated next to his boss, Janine Kysliak, who chose the destination because her husband's family was from there. The economy was on the upswing, and there was great demand for cranes and all sorts of other heavy construction equipment their firm brokered. Newfound capitalism in faraway lands was good for business as it turned out, no matter how gray and dreary these countries were.

Janine was a fair and pleasant boss, but when she got down to business she could be quite authoritative and brooked no foolishness. She clearly rose to chief operations officer on her work and determination, but no doubt her good looks contributed to the speed of her ascent. Short, closely cropped blond hair framed an alabaster face like that of a china doll, which she frequently accented with bold shades of red lipstick, delivering a slight emo vibe. Her body was enviable, the result of regular workouts in the early morning, and she tended to call attention to her best asset, her legs, with hose and professional pumps in the two- to three-inch range. At 39, she was six years Lester's junior, and where most men might resent that, he generally brushed off the age disparity, and sometimes thought back to a rather politically incorrect Jack Nicholson line from *A Few Good Men*: "There's nothing sexier than taking orders from a female officer."

For the long flight, Janine opted for leather flat-heeled boots that came to just under her knees, but still chose black nylons underneath. Lester found the look quite fetching, especially when she crossed her legs to the extent possible in the business class seat, and the weave of the nylons pulled tight across her knee. He imagined, too, that a wonderful witch's brew of odors were taking root in the feet of those boots, which is probably why she didn't attempt to remove them during the flight. Still, as one with an affinity for women's feet, he couldn't keep his mind from wandering to the thought of being in the room when she finally took those boots off.

This all made for a mostly enjoyable flight, their final destination notwithstanding.

When the plane touched down at Zhuliani Airport in Kyiv, it was just past noon local time. Jet lag was a certainty, but for now, the priority was settling into their hotel in downtown – alas, in separate rooms, so there'd be no whiff of his boss' magical cocktail. Their meetings didn't begin until the next morning, so they'd have time to rest or explore to the extent that either was up for that. A pre-arranged translator would be joining them, though Lester knew Janine could struggle through a basic conversation in Ukrainian. They parted company in the 11th floor hallway of what was actually a very nice hotel with classic European design flourishes.

Ensconced in his room, Lester surveyed the minibar and chose some peanut butter cups with Cyrillic letters but in the familiar orange package. He tested the bed but knew sleep wouldn't come to him. Also, he wanted to get a good night's rest later so he'd be refreshed and ready for some good deal-making the next day. He flipped on the TV, drank a lot of water, and leafed through the tourist guides and newspapers in the room. *Amazing there's a tourist industry here*, he marveled, *but hey, I guess people needed distractions when they come, and everybody needs to eat*. There was no shortage of happening restaurants in the area.

Flipping through a courtesy newspaper, he noticed the ads in the back for a different kind of tourism. Most were in Cyrillic, but some carried English words as well. But even without text, it was clear they were offering female companionship, typically the very busty type, and often to business travelers no doubt. Not that he'd summon an escort, but he was intrigued to see the variety of ads. Leafing now from back to front, toward the dining section, he spotted an ad that seemed to bridge both the raunchy and the epicurean. It spoke to his inner soul, in both Ukrainian and English. "The Foot Fetish Café."

Curious, he let his eyes linger on the ad, which featured three lovely young women chowing down, all barefoot. Beneath the photo it said, "The only place in Ukraine where nobody pays to eat."

That was interesting. *How do they stay in business*, he wondered. Nonetheless, the name and the picture fascinated Lester. And he was hungry. It turned out the Foot Fetish Café was a short cab ride from the hotel. *What the hell*, he thought, *I'll get a bite and maybe meet a woman who shares my interest.*

He showered to remove the filth of the long flight and put on fresh casual clothes. If it wasn't so dreary out he might've hoofed the two miles or so to the restaurant, but had the bellhop summon a green taxi instead. He gave the driver the address, without actually saying the name of the establishment. As the driver nodded, a barely perceptible smile on his lips, Lester determined he'd driven many visitors to the same café.

His mind raced during the short ride. He might have a good story to tell his guy friends back home, or maybe even learn the secret to letting patrons eat for free. He grew more excited the closer they got. With a name so blatantly explicit, he figured he was in for an experience of some kind.

The taxi let him out in front of a gray stucco building with a green awning and a tasteful sign, again in both Cyrillic and English. There were two large windows – one to either side of the ornate wooden door – but thin curtains concealed any specific activity inside from prying eyes. It almost smacked of a bordello, but this was definitely not the red light district of Kyiv.

Girding himself, Lester turned the knob and stepped inside. The interior was bright and cheerful. There was a podium in front, much like a maître de station in a classy American restaurant. Several yards away he saw some comfortable-looking banquettes with high cushioned backs and elevated on pedestals, They had built-in tray tables that appeared to fold open and closed.

An attractive woman with dark hair in a bun and piercing green eyes walked over and greeted him in English.

"Hello," Lester replied. "Um…can I please see a menu?"

"Absolutely," the woman said, handing him a tall piece of cardboard. Lester scanned it, orienting himself to the layout, words in Cyrillic and English, and price information, in both hryvnia and U.S. dollars. After a long pause, the hostess asked, "can I answer any questions?"

Lester was certain his face began to redden. The prices weren't for food. Indeed, it appeared some guests did eat for free. But for him, the pricing became quite clear.

"Uh, how exactly does this work?" Lester asked, deciding it might be fun to have this beauty walk him through it.

"It is simple. Our women patrons eat for free. The men, or some women as well – how do you say – subsidize…their meals. It is 2100 hryvnia for 30 minutes…about $75 dollars U.S."

Okay, so we guys get to pay for the women's food, he thought. *What do we get in return?*

She answered before he could ask the question she must have known was coming. "During that time you sit under the girls' feet while they enjoy their meal and their conversation."

"Uh huh," was all he could say. Had he stumbled into some kind of fantasy land? His penis began to swell, and he was thankful he was wearing roomy khakis.

Trying to maintain decorum and not sound too eager, he simply said, "I'd like one hour, um, I think."

"Of course." He paid upfront, cash in U.S., musing that he'd have to skip this one when he filed his expense report. "Right this way, sir."

The tastefully dressed hostess led him into the main dining room, and Lester enjoyed the view of her bare legs, black patent pumps and ass-hugging red skirt. He'd be quite content if she were one of the patrons during his hour here, he decided. The thought of getting something to eat himself abandoned his mind. The way his stomach was swirling, he wasn't sure he was even hungry anymore.

She stopped when they got to one of the banquettes, and she extended her arm.

"Make yourself comfortable. We have some guests arriving for a 1:30 reservation."

Lester looked down and noticed a thin padded cushion poking out from the space under the curved bench seat.

"Um, well, do I…uh, take off my clothes?"

"No, silly, stay dressed," she said with a coy smile. "But put this on, then just lie down with your upper body sticking out." She handed him a black half-balaclava that covered his face from the nose up, with generous openings at the nostrils and eyes, then deposited three menus – presumably the food kind – on the bench.

"Relax, and enjoy yourself." Her smile broadened, and Lester read much into that.

Without fully knowing what he was getting into, Lester slipped the mask over his head, adjusting it so his orifices lined up with the holes. It fit snugly, but not uncomfortably. He maneuvered into position, sliding his legs and torso under the fixture, up to just below his collar bone. He stared up, noting the ceiling tiles and the odd water stain, anticipating what lay ahead. He felt his penis stir. Whatever he was paying for – and he had a pretty good idea by this point – his manhood was already leaping for joy.

In just a couple of minutes, he heard female voices getting closer. They were speaking Ukrainian, and laughing easily as women do when they get together. He tilted his neck back and got his first, albeit upside down, look at three women walking assuredly his way, heels clicking on the floor to herald their approach. He couldn't make out too much from this angle, but they all appeared to be in their 20s, all attractive, and dressed as though they were coming from work. Perhaps they were co-workers, Lester reasoned, looking for something different on their lunch break. No doubt The Foot Fetish Café was an economical option for young office employees seeking to save a hryvnia. The hostess was leading them.

All three women glanced down at him, but only for a moment, as if he was something to avoid tripping over, then turned their attention back to each other as they sat down, smoothing out their skirts as they did so. Suddenly, Lester's head was flanked by three pairs of legs and feet. His cheeks reddened, and he was immediately hit with the scent of suede and leather, mixed with a pleasant, musky perfume.

He began to second-guess his decision-making process as the fantasy became reality. These women paid him no mind – he might have well been a speed bump. They browsed the menu, legs shifting in close proximity to his temples as they got comfortable. Momentarily, a waitress in functional black sneakers and black slacks arrived, and pleasantly took their orders. She didn't so much as bother to look down at his face.

Despite being ignored – or, more likely, because of it – his penis further swelled. Concealed from anybody's view, Lester chose to embrace it. His breathing became measured as he enjoyed the aroma wafting around his head. And whether or not they gave him a thought, Lester was now fully focused on his tormentresses. The legs closest to his left cheek were sheathed in opaque black tights with a subtle decorative weave, and belonged to a slender woman with dark hair tied in a ponytail. She had a thin nose that smoothly sloped downward and wore a tasteful shade of lipstick that nonetheless stood out against a light complexion. She was dressed in a dark gray, scoop neck, cotton dress that ended just above her knees. Black suede shoes with 4-inch heels seemed to blend with her leggings.

An inch to his right were the feet of a young woman of about 22 with dark hair and the face of a sweet girl next door, the type you'd happily hire to sit for your kids. But her outfit was more risqué than that of the typical babysitter, between a red top of angora or similarly soft fabric and a black micro-mini skirt, over sheer black stockings. It was her shoes that particularly caught Lester's attention…black, patent leather with heels of at least five inches and a delightfully enticing narrow ankle strap. He inhaled deeply and could smell that leather.

However it was the third girl, seated directly above him with her legs astride his head, that would be Lester's undoing. The long-haired blonde had a haughty expression about her, as though she came here less for the free food than the chance to lord over hapless males. Her tight black minidress hugged her lithe shape, and she wore nude hose, the right leg of which had the beginnings of a ladder on the inside. She had fetching red patent pumps with well-scuffed soles that made Lester think they'd seen many long hours on her size 7 or 8 feet. The crowning touch was a thin gold anklet dangling a small charm on her left ankle.

Lester craved a better view of her gorgeous legs, maybe a glimpse of her knees or upper thighs, but he was relegated to an ant's-eye view of the scene. Which at this point meant mainly the lower legs and shoes of all three women. And wasn't that appropriate? To these goddesses, he was little more than an insect, or maybe their meal ticket. That thought, combined with the aromas and teasingly limited view, made him fully erect, and he had no doubt he was turning redder under the mask upon realizing it. And they had only just sat down!

Thus began the most exciting 60 minutes of Lester's life.

He heard them chattering as co-workers do, frequently punctuated with laughter. They might have been talking about him and he'd never know it, but for now they continued ignoring him. Ponytail was regaling her friends with a story apparently, and their rapt attention was only broken by giggling and the occasional scoffing sound. Laughter was laughter in any language, and Lester always enjoyed the sound of young women snickering.

Girl-next-door brought her right hand down and began scratching her foot between the upper and strap of her shoe with a single, black-painted nail. Lester dared to turn his head right so he could better see the movement. She scratched persistently, and the nylon revealed some redness of the skin beneath. Her face remained focused on her friend, however, even as she began undoing the ankle strap – no doubt to gain more access to the irritating spot. The movement drew Lester's eyes almost helplessly, but at the moment she revealed her stocking foot, ponytail's suede pump pressed down on his left cheek. He made a feeble attempt to lift his head, but her foot was unyielding, and he found he now couldn't avert his gaze from girl-next-door's foot if he wanted to.

His nose was assaulted with an earthy, vinegary scent that went straight to the pleasure center of his brain. His penis spasmed in its hideaway, and he wished he'd had the foresight to undo his fly before laying down to relieve the pressure that was now his bane. Black nylon, encasing short toes and black toenails, filled his field of view and she continued rubbing, essentially giving herself a foot massage. After 30 seconds, ponytail said something amusing, all three girls chuckled, then she lifted her pump off his cheek.

Girl-next-door's stocking foot now pushed his right cheek, forcing him to look straight up, and in a swift motion she planted the same foot squarely on his face, then began moving it slowly but firmly up and down. As his lower lip curled to and fro with it and his nose was compressed with the motion, Lester surmised that the brunette told her to let their toy's face do the work her hand had been doing.

The pressure mounted, both against his face and the inside of his pants. Lest he turn his face to the side, ponytail placed her right foot firmly against his right cheek, and girl-next-door planted her left foot on his left cheek. Not that he wanted to turn his head.

It was at this point the blonde started to move her foot, placing it squarely on his forehead as if to say "don't resist." The dirty sole felt rough through the thin mask, until she deftly removed the shoe and began kneading her toes against his hairline. The stink of her freshly liberated sole assaulted his compressed nostrils. When he opened his mouth to suck in a gulp of air, girl-next-door's sensuous heel slipped in, forcing him to breath around it.

Astonishingly, the three women kept right on chatting, barely looking down at him. He found this nonchalance to be incredibly erotic; his plight was of no concern to them. He could sense the return of the waitress, and they only paused their ministrations to his head long enough to take the plates of food she handed over. He guessed they'd ordered wraps or sandwiches of some kind.

Now, the haughty blonde set both of her feet on her face, with just enough pressure to let him know she was in control but no so much that he couldn't inhale her delightful foot odor. Indeed, he felt compelled to suck in deeply, and he stole a look up at her lovely face as he did so. She was grinning toothily between bites of her food, and she began sliding her left foot up and down his face as girl-next-door had done, but not as roughly. It was methodical, and rhythmic. Between cycles, he could see the dangling portion of her ankle chain swinging. Unbidden, he stuck out his tongue and the stretched nylon encasing her foot dragged across it, up and down, up and down.

The next 15 minutes were quite literally a blur as his eyes became watery from both the abuse his face was taking and the combined foot odor, which many men would find offensive but Lester reveled in. Ponytail was the only one to keep her shoes on, and she used her high heel to good effect to enforce the will of her two friends. The mask was both a blessing and a curse; at the same time it saved his skin from some splotching that would be hard to explain later, it frustratingly limited his contact with blondie's and girl-next-door's nylon soles.

Finishing their food, the three ladies began to gather their belongings and Lester had a close-up view as two of them put their shoes back on. The blonde even used his cheeks as an anchor as she maneuvered her feet into her well-worn red stilettos, first the right shoe, then the left. As the vixens who came in here dined completely free, there was no check and no money to trifle with. All three stood, and now Lester strained for a peak up their skirts, but the dark recesses he found obscured the treasures within.

The blonde paused, looked down at his face deliberately for the first time, and smiled. "Do pobachennya," she said, her eyebrow arched derisively. Apparently a goodbye of some kind. Sensing he didn't speak the language, she followed in English with "I hope you enjoy." Lester's pulse raced at finally being acknowledged as a person. As something of a parting gift, she raised her right foot and slowly drew the scruffy sole from his forehead to his chin. He felt his erect penis throb again as all three women laughed.

Lester lay there reflecting on what he'd just been through. Although he'd lost track of time, he wasn't quite ready to get up. These women had messed with his psyche, and he couldn't instantly return to his businessman mode. And their foot odor still lingered on his mask and face, and in his head.

Around him, he vaguely saw other men taking their spots under other banquettes, females of all varieties taking their seats above them. One man was under two women; another bench had two men under two thin girls who barely looked 18. One of them popped a bubble of gum.

He heard the hostess approaching, and thought he was about to be kicked out, but instead noticed from his prone position two pairs of legs. There was an exchange in Ukrainian, although one side of the conversation was stilted, with lots of pauses.

The feet stopped a yard from his head, and one of the women sat down, legs astride his head. Fashionable black boots, nearly flat heels and ending an inch or two beneath black-nylon knees. *Oh god!* Lester thought in a panic. *It's Janine!*

With 70 percent mortification but at least 30 percent excitement, he squeezed his eyes closed tight. He would just about die if she recognized him, or if his fetish were to be exposed. How could he work with her day-to-day if she viewed him as a foot pervert? Who else might she tell? Lester's stomach churned with embarrassment, and his face beneath the mask turned bright red again. Yet in spite of the fear coursing through him, blood once again coursed through his flagging erection.

"Please," the hostess said, handing his boss a menu, "make yourself comfortable. Tatiana will be over to take your order."

Lester risked a peek through half-closed eyes. Janine's lovely face, donning an apparently fresh coat of bright red lipstick, focused on the menu, with just a scant glance down at the man whose head lay between her feet. Her tongue poked out and licked her lips as she scanned the sandwiches. His breathing became shallow, as if he was commanding his body to be as inconspicuous as possible.

Suddenly, Janine's hand reached down and began pulling down the long zipper of her right boot to free her foot from its 16-hour prison. There was actually a slight audible whoosh as the leather collapsed off her lower leg, and a redolent odor wafted through the square yard surrounding Lester's face. He inhaled deeply now – it was almost involuntary – and took in an acrid scent that struck his addled brain as a mix of sharp cheese, leather and corn chips, with a hint of vinegar. As she continued to peruse the menu, pert toes that sloped gently from her big toe to her pinky toe, and painted a deep red, wiggled vibrantly, the dance of liberation, fanning the aroma. Regardless of where her eyes were looking, their owner was no doubt blissfully aware the effect this would have after a long flight on the likes of a patron at someplace called the Foot Fetish Café.

Lester felt uncomfortable pressure against the crotch of his pants again, a spot of moisture expanding in his jockey shorts. His eyes remained slits as he heard the second zipper coming down. Momentarily, he knew, the air directly above him would become even more saturated with the aftereffects of international travel in kid-leather knee-high boots and pantyhose.

He once again breathed in deeply, his shame and fear of discovery slowly being nudged aside by his growing arousal at the impossible, delightful situation he found himself in. His every practical instinct said to stand up and run. He'd be a momentary blur, then live to fight another day. But his fetish mind held him frozen, in thrall of Janine's malodorous extremities.

As his mind darted between options, his ultimate decision was made for him as his supervisor's right foot slowly came off the floor, hovered over his face, then came down with no small amount of force. The stocking sole felt a bit gritty against his lip, soiled from the detritus from its long leather encasement. He was adjusting to the sudden warmth against his exposed skin when his peripheral vision caught Tatiana arriving to take Janine's lunch order. As she ordered in English, her left foot traced a similar arc to her right before landing on the left portion of his face. Lester was once again immobilized, and he emitted a soft groan.

Consciously or not, his boss' feet began to move over his face as blondie's had done before, only this time it distinctly felt she was simply adjusting to get comfortable. Lester suddenly felt secure, like he was where he needed to be at this moment, and even took solace in the fact that with his face as Janine's literal foot stool, it was much less likely she'd recognize him.

Her soles continued to rasp against his face as her order arrived and she ate. With no meetings until the morning, she seemed to be in no hurry at all, even ordering a second glass of wine. All the while, Lester took in the intoxicating, fiendish smell. *It would be a very interesting flight home*, he thought, inhaling deeply again. *Very interesting indeed.*

Adjusted

Finley Rayburn sat in the comfortable molded chair of his chiropractor's office, waiting to be admitted to one of the treatment rooms for his weekly adjustment. He didn't mind the wait. He sipped from a cup of hot green tea, a regular perk, and he quite enjoyed the view of the three young ladies who helmed the front desk, who served as both reception/clerical staff and chiropractic assistants. All under 30, they had grabbed his attention the first time he came in following a car crash in which he was rear-ended. The driver fled the scene, no less, only to be arrested later, but he was left with some whiplash that radiated throughout his upper body. And to hear the doctor tell it, his spinal column was out-of-whack too. There was a lawsuit pending.

He'd been referred to the office of Ultimate Chiropractic by his mother-in-law Nadine, after she had strained her back doing some dance move or other with one of her many suitors. That's what you get when you hit the dance floor at age 62 in stiletto leopard-print heels, he thought at the time. Still, he had to admit she probably looked great doing it. She could still rock a short skirt and heels at her age, and who could begrudge her a little fun? "They treat you like family there," she'd said of the practice several months before while sitting in their living room, as she crossed one glorious leg over the other, distracting him from her words.

The endorsement was ironic, as she'd never really treated *him* like family. She always seemed to only tolerate him, even in his own home, as though she was perennially disappointed her daughter had married beneath her. And after nine years without granting Nadine a grandchild, she somehow thought he was to blame, despite the fact it was a mutual choice, not a biological impediment. She was frequently downright dismissive of him, but Finley let it roll off his shoulder mainly because he loved his wife and, truth be told, her imperious mien toward him tended to arouse him a little bit.

When he arrived that first day, Jessica, the dark-haired assistant, had conducted his intake exam, and he'd been temporarily able to forget his pain at the close proximity as she scanned his bare back from the coccyx to the cervical vertebrae in his neck. He had on one of those loose hospital gowns and was otherwise clothed, but his mind wandered pleasantly as her fingernails made occasional contact, and at the musky scent of her perfume. A bright smile with perfect teeth further distracted him as they conducted the initial appointment. Today, she wore tasteful pleated beige linen slacks, a white blouse, and black ballet flats.

Her colleagues, Meghan and Sabrina, were also clad professionally as they went about their work. Meghan, a redhead of about 24, had a slender nose, thin lips with very modest gloss, and pleasant hazel eyes. Sabrina, who favored a bit more makeup, sported wavy shoulder-length brown hair, high cheekbones and cute dimples which emerged every time she smiled, which was often. Indeed, as Nadine had said, all three were unfailingly pleasant whenever they dealt with clients of the practice. And after a couple of months coming in, Finley enjoyed flirting with all three of them, despite the ring on his finger.

Their employer, Maritza, was a statuesque, amber-haired beauty with eyes that looked like they'd been drawn by a manga artist. Nearly six feet tall, she was well-toned and her upper body in particularly looked hewn by frequent workouts, or the demands of her profession, or more likely both. The owner of the practice and its only doctor, at 35 she looked far younger than what Finley would expect from an accomplished medical professional. She too was ebullient with patients, and unlike the office staff, she was prone to wearing skirts, which highlighted her sculpted, always tan legs, often set off by strappy sandals which revealed delightfully polished toes. She was the main reason he looked forward to his visits, partly to admire her form and partly to be laying flat on his stomach on the adjustment table as she manipulated him, with both her strong hands and the "activator," a small device that looked a bit like a corkscrew but applied strategic pressure to key points in increments of $1/10,000^{th}$ of a second.

He would lay on that table waiting for her to bounce into the room, letting his mind wander about what else she might be able to do to him with her well-honed knowledge of the human anatomy. And it didn't escape his attention that the table itself looked like it was designed more for pleasure than any kind of therapy. Like a massage table, it had an opening wide enough for the patient to rest their face flat, with their nose sticking through, as an adult's ankles hung off the end. But this table's two-inch wide opening ran nearly the length of its surface, ostensibly to accommodate children or smaller individuals. Finley couldn't help thinking what other protuberances that slot could accommodate.

His mind raced with such thoughts, but even if he became physically aroused during the 10-minute sessions, it would be discreet as the table's overhanging sidewalls would shield any impropriety from casual viewers. So he never worried as he fantasized or snuck peeks at Maritza's pretty feet as she worked him over.

On this day, however, he had other plans. Maybe it was the gleam in Jessica's eye when he checked in, or maybe the fact he hadn't gotten any sex from his wife in more than two weeks due to her travel schedule for work. Maybe it was simply that he wanted to do something that would scare the heck out of him, and that he could think about later, alone, that evening.

Finley typically waited about five minutes once he was prone on the table. Today, he unzipped. He didn't even have to get up to do it, just maneuvered his fly open where he lay and, as discreetly as possible, manipulated his manhood through the slot in the table. To all outward appearances, he was just another patient laying on his stomach awaiting treatment. But his lower stomach tingled with excitement at his little secret and he felt his mouth going dry.

"Finley, how you doing today?" said Maritza as she bounded into the room. "How's that body feeling?"

"I'm great, Doc. How are you?" His voice didn't betray what he was doing below his waist.

"Another great day. Let's see what we've got going on!"

With that she began narrating her activity as it concerned his neck and lower back. She always explained these things, but Finley seldom understood what she was talking about. All he knew was her ministrations were making him feel better with each passing week. After two or three minutes she said, cheery as could be, "OK, let's turn you over and have a look at that pelvis."

Finley thought he didn't hear her right. "Um, what?

"Turn onto your back. You've graduated."

"I, um…" He stammered. "You always just do the back."

"It's a big day, Finley, moving onto the next phase of treatment."

Finley's face reddened. There'd be no way to hide his indiscretion, nor any plausible way to explain it away. His cheeks became numb, and he remained immobilized. "I, uh…"

Maritza placed her hands on her hips, starting to lose patience but in the most pleasant of ways. "Is there a problem?"

Finley sucked in a gulp of air. This was an impossible situation, one that he couldn't easily escape. His mind one again raced, but this time with the goal of self-preservation. Seeing no easy out, he whispered, "Uh, can I, uh have a moment?"

Maritza's face exhibited a look of sudden realization. "Hey, look, it's alright…believe me, physical responses to treatment are not unusual. Nothing to worry about, I am a doctor after all."

Her words were meant to be reassuring, but they did nothing to mitigate Finley's overwhelming sense of shame at his predicament. Natural arousal was one thing. Your cock sticking through the adjustment table in all its glory was quite another. He tensed as the doctor grasped his shoulders to encourage him to roll over.

"Wait! Wait!" He girded himself, and felt his eyes literally moisten at the fate about to befall him. She removed her hands, and with no way to hide his motions he tried desperately to tuck himself back in. But there was only so much he could do without standing up. He stared straight at the ceiling as he turned on his back, his fly as open as a barn door and his shirt tail poking through. No, there'd be no explaining.

"What's going on here?" Maritza asked, with a distinct mix of surprise and accusation. *I'm done*, Finley thought.

"It's uh, nothing, really. I just needed to – " he paused, trying to frame the words, the lie, in his head, "relieve some pressure when I laid down on the table. Tight jeans. I was uncomfortable."

Maritza nodded slowly, outwardly appearing to buy the story. But Finley somehow knew she didn't.

"Maybe we should resume your adjustment next week. I'll leave you to…" her words trailed off as she stepped out of the room.

Finley stood up, mortified, and hastily zipped up. He'd never been caught in such a state. *Damn me*, he thought, *now I'm the practice perv*. Could he ever return? Multiple thoughts passed through his head. She's a professional, he reasoned, and has probably seen everything. She'll get past it, maybe even forget it ever happened. She certainly won't ever *mention* it again, of that he was sure. So that laid the burden on him. Could his dignity survive this? He flashed forward to the distant future and saw himself laughing about it, maybe sharing the story with a buddy over a beer. *We'll see if that happens*, he thought hopefully.

He grabbed his jacket, and without even putting it on against the chilly weather, strode out of the office, without so much as casting a glance at or saying goodbye to the ladies at the desk.

Finley's head swam during the ensuing week, but he was paid up for a year's worth of treatments, so knew he'd be returning. He girded himself for his next visit, telling himself that the doctor was, in fact, a professional. It was highly doubtful she'd share his indiscretion with anyone.

When he arrived at Ultimate Chiropractic the following week, Jessica greeted him pleasantly as per usual, and offered a cup of green tea, which he accepted. From his vantage point in the waiting area, he noticed she had on a suede skirt today, in a bit of a departure from her usual attire, and fetching black ankle boots. He felt relaxed, both from the hot tea and the realization that just maybe nothing was out of the ordinary. The tea was soothing to his throat and settled his stomach. He stared out the large windows at the snow that had just begun falling outside. A warmth overcame him, an almost giddy feeling. After a few minutes, his eyes began to close.

"Wake up, Finley."

"Huh?" He must've gone out while waiting. He felt like he was outside himself, but still very relaxed. He lifted his head, only then realizing he was lying down. *No*, he thought, *I couldn't have fallen onto the floor*. He didn't feel hard tiles beneath him. He was…comfortable.

"That's it, wake up. You're in the adjustment room."

It was Maritza's voice. He brought his right hand to his face and rubbed his eyes. He raised his head to get his bearings, a new sense of embarrassment overtaking him as he realized he must've fallen asleep in the waiting room. That had never happened to him anywhere before. He was confused, but began to orient himself as he looked up at the doctor standing at his 11 o'clock. She wore navy blue slacks, a light blue, loose-fitting blouse, and laceless gray sneakers.

"I, um, I'm sorry," he muttered. He tried to raise himself up to a sitting position, but was stopped short by a sharp yank below his belt. What the hell? This didn't compute. Why couldn't he get up?

"You seem to be saying that a lot lately. By the way, Nadine says hello."

Nadine? Now he was thoroughly confused. "Huh? What the – ?" He shuffled his body on the adjustment table, but couldn't move more than an inch laterally before feeling the pressure around his private parts again. He stopped his shuffling. "What do you mean? What's going on?"

"I guess you didn't know that your mother-in-law and I have stayed in touch since her treatment, we actually have a lot of things in common. She's something else."

Finley began to worry. "Not sure what you're getting at, Maritza."

"We talk about everything, Finley." She said this with a mischievous grin. "Everything."

Oh shit. "Oh no…" he muttered.

"Oh yes."

Finley pulled upward again but his ball sac again pulled him back laying flat on his stomach. He tried to reach under the table to address the problem but his hands could only move so far due to the table's sideboards. He stopped moving as Maritza summoned Jessica and Sabrina. The two employees entered, both smiling broadly, eyes wide as they looked at him.

"You can't get up, Finley. While you were out I put a collar around your testicles. Last week you wanted to stick your penis through the opening…so now you're stuck through," she giggled, prompting the spectators to laugh as well. "Nadine thought you needed to learn a lesson, and frankly, I was happy to oblige. That was very disrespectful, Finley. Think of this as…another adjustment, only this time it's an attitude adjustment."

Another round of laughter. His face reddened, and fear rose up inside of him. *If Nadine knows what I did, then I'm screwed*, Finley thought.

Noticing his concerned look, Maritza said, "Don't worry, Finley. She wants this to be our little secret."

This can't be happening. This was a medical office, after all. He struggled again, in the hope of regaining some amount of dignity, but he only caused himself pain.

"Jessica."

Bending down, Jessica picked up what looked to be a red dog leash which he hadn't noticed. She sat down in one of the observation chairs and in doing so pulled it taut. The yank on his sac quickly immobilized him.

"Youch!"

"I told you, you should just relax."

With the doctor standing behind him out of sight, he now focused on Sabrina, who sat down on the floor with her legs tucked under the table. He hadn't really noticed how attractive she was before now. While looking into his face, and with some ceremony, she squeezed some oil into her left hand. *No, she wouldn't*, Finley thought. *There's no way.*

He sucked in his breath as Sabrina began stroking him, and his cock, which was never anything but flaccid since this began, started to inflate. He sighed deeply at her up-and-down ministrations. He willed himself to remain soft so as not to give them their satisfaction, but his body refused to cooperate. Glancing over at Jessica, he saw her chin resting on the hand holding the leash, a stoic expression on her face. It was almost as if she was deep in thought. For some reason, this turned him on further.

After just a few minutes of long, slow strokes, Finley felt like he was about to climax and, sensing this, Sabrina loosened her grip. He sucked in a breath and released it in a quiet moan. He didn't know what their plan was for him, but for now he just decided to give in and enjoy the sensations. When he collected himself, her slow, tight stroking resumed.

After just a few more maddening up-and-down cycles, there was a knock on the practice door. Maritza excused herself, and momentarily Finley heard talking in the distance. He became petrified that another patient or someone else had arrived, and might catch a glimpse of what was going on. *But surely the practice was closed*, he thought, *they must've locked the front door*. That provided a sense of relief that turned out to be very short-lived.

"We're so glad you were able to make it after all," Maritza sang.

No, Finley thought. *It can't be*. He planted his face down in despair, his nose poking through the slot of the table.

"Look who's joined us! Say hello, Finley. Don't be rude."

With his temples starting to throb as much as his penis was down below, Finley quickly raised his eyes to see his mother-in-law walk in the room. He buried his head back in the soft table just as fast, and felt Sabrina's hand speeding up just a bit at that moment. He groaned.

"Well, it seems like he's a little…preoccupied," Nadine said. "Can't say I blame him. Sabrina, dear, you have a marvelous technique."

"Thanks, Nadine," Sabrina replied, casting a big smile in her direction.

Finley sucked in the familiar scent of his mother-in-law, a bit like roses mixed with fruitiness. How could this have happened, he wondered, as he heard her shuffle into the chair to Jessica's right, along the wall to his left. He heard a faint hissing sound of nylon against nylon as she crossed her legs in a movement that never failed to capture his attention. Only this time, he couldn't bring himself to look.

Sabrina's hands were now tickling his balls, and Finley again moaned. "Please don't," he managed to mutter. Despite the wonderful sensations, he now deeply feared that he would lose control in front of his *bête noir*, not just random, albeit very attractive, medical staff. His psyche devolved into the depths of shame, and he just wanted this to end, orgasm or no. He worried what his wife would say if god forbid Nadine told her about this. He feared his mother-in-law would hold this over him, to assert control over his life. "Stop, please let me leave," his voice protested, but the thoughts swirling in his head made him grow even harder.

"Quiet down, Finley, and take it like a man," Nadine snapped. "Or else my daughter will have to hear all about this…every last detail."

Suitably chastened, he let the softness of Sabrina's oiled hand wash over him. She was now palming the head, and he was becoming unglued. His hands flailed in a futile attempt to stop the treatment…or speed up the relief his body now desperately sought.

"May I dear?" Nadine asked of Jessica, nodding down to the end of the leash in her hand.

"Of course!" she said, placing the loop in Nadine's manicured hand.

"Look at me, Finley," Nadine said quietly. She gave a slight tug to get his attention.

He moaned, then slowly turned his head to the left. It was only now that he could take in the entire tableau. His mother-in-law wore a silky blouse with a pattern of multi-color squares, complemented by a short black skirt. Casting a quick glance down, he noticed she had on the beige hose she appeared to favor, and a devastating pair of black patent Casadei Blades with their trademark five inch, gently tapering heels. *Damn*, he thought, *for a woman in her early 60s, she was incredibly enticing.*

He felt his penis start to spasm, and like a pro Sabrina abruptly pulled her hand away. Finley turned his face down into the table and whimpered.

"No, Finley, look at me," the older woman sang, giving a slightly sharper yank on the strap. Finley's balls cried out, and he again turned his head to the side. After a good 20 seconds, Sabrina resumed her slow up-and-down stroking, grazing her fingernails against his balls on each downstroke.

"I…I'm sorry…this isn't…" But he couldn't complete the thought.

"Here, Nadine, lift up your foot," Maritza said leaning down and taking the strap from her hand. She looped it around the older woman's nylon-encased ankle. "Now if he looks away, just drag your foot under the chair. Instant compliance!" She laughed, and even the stone-faced Jessica chuckled.

"That will work," Nadine said. She tested the set-up, dragging her left heel a few inches backward. Her motion tugged at the donut surrounding Finley's balls.

"Yeouw!" He started to pant, in spite of Sabrina's hand working him over. "You bitch!" He pressed his face back into the cushioned table. Through the slot, he saw the fingers dancing over his penis, the pleasure of his masturbatrix's movements at odds with his sudden pain.

"Finley! I think you should be more respectful of your mother-in-law," Maritza said, with a sneer in her voice, "seeing as she literally has you by the balls." All three women again chuckled.

"I'm sorry," he gasped into the vinyl cushion. "I'm sorry."

"Look at my face when you say it, Finley," Nadine said, her lips curving up in a smirk, "or I will yank you with my foot."

He turned his head and with great effort brought his eyes to meet hers. What he saw there chilled him, and excited him at the same time. A look of disdain, like contempt but with a mild show of joy. His every fiber urged him to look away, but he didn't want to risk more torment to his balls. His breathing settled down, as he became more docile to the commanding woman who occupied his view. "I – I'm sorry, Nadine."

"How's he doing, Sabrina?" Maritza asked.

"He's getting all gooey," she responded as her soft hand made circles around his frenulum.

"Use some more oil, dear," Nadine chimed in, sliding the tube over with her beautifully shod left foot.

Barely missing a stroke, Sabrina lubed her right hand then rubbed them together, working it in. The faint squishing sound excited Finley. She now rolled his hardness between both hands as if making a snake out of clay. Finley moaned loudly, his eyes still locked on his mother-in-law's smug face.

He tried to command his body to resist, in a bid to retain some dignity and a desire to not let these women win. He tensed his legs, and his body bucked, trying desperately to avoid a shameful episode. Noticing this movement, Nadine again pulled her right foot backward, her high heel scraping loudly on the wood laminate flooring, bringing the cord taut. Finley winced.

"Be still, Finley," Nadine cooed. "I wouldn't want to tell Sarah about your inappropriate activity at the chiropractor's office."

The threat loomed large, and had the desired effect on him. His body settled. Whatever these women were doing paled compared to his fate if his wife found out about his initial infraction.

His ball sac pulled tight, he now felt Sabrina's fingertips playing across them, and it was maddening. At the same time, her other hand began stroking his length more slowly, but with a very firm grip. He afforded himself a glance downward at Nadine's hosed legs, the right one with the leash looped around the ankle and the left crossed over on top, the nylon pulled tight on her knee and shining in the fluorescent overhead light so that he could nearly make out the strands of fabric. Her shoes gleamed as well, the visible scuffed red sole of her left shoe making a stark and sexy contrast with the black patent leather. His mouth was dry, and in spite of himself, he moaned again.

"Look at me," Nadine reminded him. He brought his eyes back up to her face. Her high cheekbones had always given her face an exquisite look; now her cheeks were sucked in and her lips pouted in an affect of sympathy, but Finley knew she was anything but sympathetic to his plight.

No one said anything as Sabrina brought him to the edge, paused, then repeated the slow, firm stroking. In his peripheral vision he could see Jessica, sitting next to his mother-in-law, now leaning forward with her chin resting on her fist, seemingly bored by what was unfolding two feet away. He felt Maritza's hand making circles on his denim-encased rear.

He hazarded another glance downward at Nadine's legs, where her left shoe now dangled from the tips of her toes as she gently rocked her leg. A hint of her dark red toenail polish became visible through the web of the nylon. That was Finley's undoing, and he moaned louder. Simultaneously, she drew her right foot back, and once again put in his place by that nefarious leash, he again focused on her pretty, albeit wrinkled, face. He'd almost rather die than admit it out loud, but she was a lovely older woman, he thought. She arched her right eyebrow and sucked in her cheeks as she sneered back at him.

Under the table, Sabrina's hand had mastered his cock. His will broken, his climax rose within him and he once again shuddered. His eyes darting between Nadine's face and the Casadei thwapping against her heel, Finley felt spurt after spurt surge out of him, causing Sabrina to rear back and evoking appreciative gasps from Jessica and Maritza. He grunted involuntarily, no longer in control of his bodily functions and throwing pride to the wind in service to the pleasure and shame that engulfed him. As he was thoroughly drained, he saw his mother-in-law merely smiling at him. She relaxed her right foot and his cock and balls hung limply under the table, now dribbling onto the floor.

"Let's get you cleaned up, Finley," Maritza said. "We still have a scheduled adjustment to do."

The Executrix

It would be a run-of-the-mill reading of the will, thought Myles Hillman, although the sums involved were anything but. Gertrude Langhorne left this earth flush with cash. The heiress to a sporting goods supply company and part-owner of a successful NFL team, she'd accumulated vast wealth while hardly ever working a day in her life. As the probate lawyer for the estate, Myles had met the decedent a few times, and was impressed how down-to-earth she was despite her money. She'd had an easy smile and laugh, and even for a septuagenarian still was blessed with a lovely face and a body most 40-year-old women would envy. Money bought a lot of help in that department, he mused, and she'd always worn the finest clothes designed to bring out her best assets.

Myles was an experienced attorney, and owed his success to being a by-the-book operator, while trying to remain affable and unflappable. This field was flush with emotions; he found that by taking a true "counselor" approach at a very difficult time in peoples' lives he garnered a lot of trust. That translated to good word-of-mouth, and business was good. A slightly heavy-set, gentlemanly type of 56 years, he wore his weight well – Gertrude wasn't the only one who knew the effect of a well-cut suit – and he still claimed most of his own hair, even if it was marching toward full-on, distinguished silver. A broad face and equally big smile helped draw people in, a good trait for a lawyer.

Mrs. Langhorne's family would arrive shortly. In-person will readings weren't just rituals seen in creepy movies; they still happened quite frequently, especially among upper-crust families.

Everyone had a keen interest in the distribution of the late loved one's wealth, and for many, it softened the blow of the loss. Indeed, Myles observed, they frequently looked forward to the passing of their dear relative.

At precisely noon, family members began streaming into his lengthy conference room. There were Gertrude's three children, a couple of their spouses, two or three cousins, and a surviving younger sister, who appeared to share the deceased's good genes. Francesca Langhorne-Hughes, sporting a slim green dress, matching suede three-inch pumps, and wrists bedecked in silver, had her own daughter, Erika Hughes, in tow. Myles knew no one except his client's children, but introductions were made and he could surmise the relationships from listening to their chit-chat, none of which directly expressed sadness about dear Gertrude.

As he typically did, Myles had laid out a spread of finger foods for his guests, and almost everyone partook. As he went for yet another wedge of cheese, the door flew open sharply and his mouth went agape. Striding in buoyantly was a raven-haired young woman, no more than 20, wearing a polka dot sleeveless top that cut off at her midriff and a tight-fitting pair of denim shorts, strategically ripped, and revealing legs that seemed unnaturally long, as though someone had Photoshopped them onto her. Her tantalizing outfit was completed by five-inch rope-wedge heels. Oddly, the first thing that came to Myles' mind was that Daisy Duke had nothing on this girl, except maybe cowboy boots.

As she traipsed across the room greeting relatives who seemed a bit stunned to see her, Myles' eyes were drawn to those wedges, and particularly the perfectly polished toes peeking out. He considered himself something of a connoisseur of women's feet, and these were perfection. Nestled perfectly on the one-inch platform of the shoe, they tapered from big toe to pinky in a smooth descent. They wore a shade that could be described as coral pink – not too hot and not too muted – and they gleamed as if she'd just come from a pedicure. Myles tongue unconsciously traversed his upper lip.

After a few moments admiring her body, muscular bare legs and those delectable feet, and listening to other members of the family greet her with everything ranging from forced pleasantries to outright scorn, Myles approached, putting out his hand.

"Hello, I'm Myles Hillman, the executor of Gertrude's estate. And you are?"

"Hi, Mr. Executor, I'm Sonia Hughes, the great niece. We gonna get this show on the road, or what?" She snapped the gum in her mouth.

Her impetuousness took him aback. There was a rhythm to these rituals, one she clearly couldn't concern herself with.

"Um, we'll be proceeding shortly. Why don't you grab something to –" but she'd already turned her back to him, presenting a stellar view of her rear end, the loose threads of her jean shorts dangling against her tan thighs. With no clue about her history, he could nonetheless tell right away why she was being coldly greeted by the other relatives. But in spite of her bratty demeanor, or possibly because of it, Myles felt a stir in the pit of his stomach. If nothing else, Ms. Sonia Hughes' presence would make the proceedings a little more…interesting as far as he was concerned.

Ten minutes later the key players were seated around the large conference table, with the remaining relatives in chairs along the wall. Myles noticed Sonia took the closest one to the front along the wall to his left, apparently eager to make her presence known. As he organized the files in front of him, he found his eyes being repeatedly drawn to those legs and wedge heels. Her thighs glimmered in the light from the overhead fluorescents, and Myles sucked in a breath when she crossed her left leg over her right. While auspiciously shuffling paperwork, he now focused on the gray, grimy sole of her left shoe. This type of shoe had a distinctively shaped footprint, tapering delicately from the wide ball of the foot to the narrow heel. He spied a bit of detritus stuck to the bottom, a dark splotch here, an errant thread or hair there.

He shifted his gaze back to his other guests, only to catch a marvelous view of Francesca smoothing her skirt as she sat down in the front right swivel chair at the table, her own glorious legs and suede heels on full display. Finding no quarter, he decided he needed to focus on the papers in his hand – the will – but it actually took a lot of will to do so.

After a short preamble in which he explained his role, the law, and some basics of probate – all recited by heart – Myles dove into the will itself. Several dry pages listing organizations she was bequeathing sums of money to, then a noticeable perking up of ears and widening of eyes when he began running down the litany of relatives in line for chunks of dear, departed Gertrude's estate. Everyone was there for one thing and one thing only: to learn how much their jackpot would be, how soon they would retire, how quickly they could put a down payment on a new, sporty car.

With no personal stake in the matter, Myles droned on. A few minutes in, he noticed Sonia's left wedge slip off her heel, and she began flapping it against her gorgeous, wrinkled arch as if she were bored, or impatient, or both. Pausing mid-sentence in his oration, he again licked his lips, re-gathered his concentration, and forged ahead.

But the thwapping of rope heel against young female flesh continued unabated. Indeed, like a metronome with its weight slid down near the bottom of the pendulum, its speed increased, causing him no small degree of distraction. It was a back-and-forth now clearly indicative of impatience, as pretty Sonia waited to hear her name mentioned. He stole a glance at those luscious pink-painted toenails as they appeared and disappeared from view with each cycle.

Myles' words caught in his throat and he cleared it, then took a sip of water. Having familiarized himself with the contents of the will well before today, he knew she was waiting for something that wouldn't come. This pained him; such beauty deserved to be recognized, rewarded, no matter how impertinent its owner might be, he thought. It was the natural order of things. Sonia would slide well into the role of heiress, shot-caller, independently wealthy debutante, he mused as he tried to mentally tamp down the disturbance growing in the front of his pants.

He continued reading the legal document, and each family member in turn let out a small gasp when he or she heard their name, hugging a spouse or clutching the hand nearest to them. But the smack of gum popping summoned his attention back to Sonia, whose dark brown eyes now were laser focused on him. Though he knew intellectually he had not personally wronged her, he oddly began to feel guilty, as if he was somehow deserving of her building wrath. A woman like this was not used to being denied anything, and here he was denying her everything.

Soon, the meeting wrapped up, and newly minted millionaires hugged each other goodbye, with promises to get together soon. Myles had heard it all before, and doubted they'd follow through. Poor Sonia lingered, putting up a pleasant face, but the probate lawyer could tell she was seething inside. She'd been officially excised from her dear departed's will, and she'd likely be exiled from the beneficiaries too. Myles felt bad for her, wished he could do something about it, give that lovely face a real reason to smile, give those gorgeous legs some added bounce in their step, but it wasn't up to him.

As he nibbled on leftovers and nodded goodbye to the Langhorne-Hughes clan, he noticed Sonia remained, as if in no particular hurry. Made sense, he thought. All the others were probably rushing out to start buying, or at least partake in a champagne fueled meal at a nice restaurant. She had no such plans.

"And how are you doing, dear?" Myles asked, with legitimate concern in his voice. Her brown eyes – this is the first moment he really noticed them – seemed to drill into him. Sparkling, with a mischievous glint. He quickly looked down, catching a prime view of her perfectly pedicured feet in the wedges.

"This was a sham, Mr. Execu-TOR," she said, drawing out the last syllable in a sneer that he actually found sexy. She sucked in her cheeks. "My great aunt loved me!"

"I, uh, I'm afraid I can't speak to that, I can only present what was in the will. I am sorry." He looked back at her face as he said it, but again quickly averted his gaze against the boiling whirlpools that were her eyes. This time, he glanced at the cleavage poking up above her halter top.

Sonia put her hands on her waist. "Well, this isn't going to stand. I visited her at least twice a year, when most of my cousins couldn't be bothered. So, I got into some trouble…who doesn't?" She paused, biting her lower lip. "This can be fixed." As she said it, her right shoe began rubbing her left calf.

Myles' gaze was drawn to the movement. She had a nice tan, too, he observed, which contrasted nicely against the cream color of the rope sandals. The room was empty now, and he allowed his eyes to linger.

"Are you even listening to me, Mr. Execu-TOR? What's your plan to fix this?"

Chastised, he snapped his eyes back up to her face, where he caught a slight smile appear on her glossy lips.

"Yes, I, um, I hear you, Ms. Hughes, but I don't think – "

"Yeah, you don't think, that's the problem. You're just a robot reading a piece of paper, huuuuh?" the last word elongated with a bitchy, childish tone. "I'm surprised you had the attention span to even do that. I saw you looking at me. Maybe you'd like to take a picture? It'd last longer." Her right forefinger glided down to the cuff of her jean shorts, and ever-so-slowly began sliding it up higher on her thigh.

Myles became discombobulated. "I'm not sure what you're getting at. I did what I'm paid to do. I think you should – "

"That the best you can do, Mr. Execu-TOR? Look, I'll make this easy for your little pea-brain. Revise the will so I get my cut. You know and I know it's what Aunt Gertrude wanted."

"With all respect, um, if it's what she wanted, I'm afraid it would've been in the will." He sucked in a breath as she drew closer to him. Her hair smelled like lilacs.

"We don't always express the things we want explicitly, but you should know that," she whispered. "There's something that you want, I'm sure." She now coyly rubbed one foot over the other. At the same time, her hand reached down and cupped his genitals, as she looked right into his eyes. "I'm willing to bet it's feet, like pink-polished, sweaty, sandaled feet to be exact."

She felt a twitch in her hand and her eyes widened. "Oh, Mr. Execu-TOR just confirmed what he wants! Now, he just needs to show little Sonia what her Great Aunt Gertrude wanted."

"Really, Ms. Hughes, there's nothing I can – oomph!" as she squeezed his testicles.

"Aww, it's the 'sweaty' part that does it for you, huuuh?? I think you should get on the floor…that's something you can do…and I suspect it's something you want to do."

Trembling, Myles dropped to his knees, relieving himself of her grip. An encouraging push on his chest by that rope sandal had him flat on his back.

"Ooh, I think Mr. Execu-TOR likes this view, doesn't he," she cooed, looking first at his crotch, then into his eyes. She licked her lips gloriously. "Unbuckle my wedge, now."

Myles obeyed, happily but with a show of reluctance. "Now the other one."

The moment her right foot was set free, she placed it on his penis, grinding as if putting out a cigarette butt. Myles gasped, then groaned.

"What's that? You'd like me to do that again?"

Despite himself, he briskly nodded his head. She repeated the motion, and a wet spot formed on his pants. At the same time, she hovered her left foot over his face. Sonia delighted in hearing him inhale deeply. Looking at the rapture on his face, she said one word. "Lick." She enforced her command by twisting her right foot again in its strategic location.

The lawyer stuck his tongue out and Sonia slid her high-arched foot back and forth, back and forth, until it was slimy with his saliva. He noticed the paleness of her sole stood in a nice contrast from her tan lower leg. He could see too that whenever she flexed that sole, deep wrinkles formed, and this excited Myles to no end.

"You like that," she whispered, now sliding her right foot more gently over the bulge below his belt. "Good boy…good executor."

After 30 more seconds of licking, Sonia determined it was time to ratchet things up.

"Take off your pants, quickly."

Myles didn't hesitate, spurred on by the tone of her voice and the sneer on her lovely face. And, quite simply, because he craved more direct contact with that gorgeous foot. His addled brain didn't realize at that moment that like the practice of law, everything was transactional, and there'd be a cost attached. But that rational part of his mind was subdued by the prospect of intense pleasure. He sighed deeply as he freed his genitals, and Sonia lightly dragged her coral pink toenails down his cock, then back the other way, slightly catching on the rim of his frenulum. She repeated the motion several times, then paused so he could tend once again to her left foot.

And he did just that with vigor, this time while she held her foot still.

"Get in between the toes, Mr. Execu-TOR. Let them know how much you love them." She giggled at the absurdity of the tableau.

Momentarily, she sat down on the floor, forcing his legs wide apart and positioning herself between them. While reinstalling her left foot over his lapping tongue, she took his six-inch cock in her satiny-soft left hand and slowly began stroking it. Her method was designed to drive him out of his mind, twisting her wrist at the top of each stroke. Her pinky nail tickled his balls on every other downstroke. She did this over and over again with practiced efficiency. Myles groaned loudly beneath her foot, inspiring her to press down harder.

His penis throbbed in her hand, and at this moment she knew she had him exactly where she wanted him.

"So what's my share of the estate, Myles?" calling him by his proper name for the first time. She lifted her left foot so he could answer.

He sighed, trying to summon an ounce of resistance. "I can't do that…if I change a word, I can be disbarred," he said, moaning again as her grip on him became more firm. "Your whole family heard the will…"

Sonia now put her right foot on his face, completely covering his eyes. It was a hot day today, and she knew their combined dampness – not to mention their odor – would have the expected effect on someone so enamored with the female foot. She sped up the stroking, intermittently playing her nails in a circular motion around the head of his cock. She felt pre-cum on her palm.

"I think you can do *something*," she replied softly, her hand bringing him ever closer to the edge of the explosion she knew he desperately wanted.

The probate attorney wanted to resist, needed to resist, but her ministrations were getting the best of him. Feebly, he said "I really can't."

Sonia pulled her hand away as Myles' penis twitched, sending a pathetic stream of milky fluid rolling down his cock. She scooped it up and wiped it on her jean shorts. His hips bucked as he tried fruitlessly to reestablish some kind of friction.

"Wrong answer, Mr. Execu-TOR," she said, grinding her soles more firmly against his face.

"Please…please don't stop."

"Oh, but you're not playing ball with me, even though I'm playing with your balls. Isn't everything a negotiation, hmmm?"

Myles' will was breaking. He really did care about his law license, really wanted to preserve his career, but he absolutely *needed* to shoot his load. Sensing his turmoil, Sonia turned the screw further.

"Look, you have two choices right now. You can revise the will and cut me in for half a mil, and gloriously shoot your cum all over this fancy conference room. Or, I can leave right now, tell all my friends and the rest of my family that you assaulted me when everyone left. I have the, um, evidence on my shorts." She playfully bestowed three more slow strokes on his cock to emphasize her threat, causing him to twitch violently.

"Either way, you could face discipline from the state bar." She giggled. "So you might as well choose option A and have the cum of your pathetic little lifetime."

Her demeaning, spoiled tone of voice, the threat, the humiliating way she spoke to him and her chuckling were his undoing. The tiny rational part of his mind still functioning actually thought, *what the hell, it's not my money.*

"Yes, yes, half a million! I'll do the paperwork before you leave! Just please, keep stroking me!"

A broad smile formed on Sonia's face, one Myles couldn't see as she alternately rubbed her left and right foot up and down his face with glee. She once again gripped his purple, throbbing member and resumed the stroking with the wrist twist at the top. It wouldn't take long, she knew. She could get on with her day, and the rest of her life.

"Good boy," she sang softly. "Shoot for your executrix." She smiled at her own wit, her slender hand pulling him closer and closer to the inevitable. "This is your career opportunity."

It took just two more strokes until Myles' hips began to buck again. Her delightfully aromatic feet pressed down hard, nearly crushing his nose, stifling his ability to breath, and keeping his upper body pinned to the floor.

"That's it," she purred. "Let it go for your executrix." With that last word Myles first dribbled, then shot long ropes of cum into the air, at least one spurt landing on Sonia's Daisy Dukes, traversing both the denim and the tan flesh peaking through a rip. She heard him suck in a gulp of her foot scent as four more spasms left a mess on the conference room carpet.

"It's Sonia Hughes," she reminded him as she stood up, "S-O-N-I-A." She reached for one of the expensive ballpoint pens on the table, and tossed it on Myles' chest. "Your executrix is waiting."

The Arrival Home

"You're late…very late."

Richard Landon hadn't even trudged his chilled bones out of the vestibule when his wife began railing into him. He was expecting to face her fury, but thought he'd at least be able to get into a warm shower first, or change into comfortable clothes.

"Do you know how embarrassed I am that my friends were left waiting for me? Tonight, of all nights! You know how annoyed I am??"

Richard wanted to blurt out that he'd just walked several miles, that his feet were killing him, that his car and his cell phone had both died at an inopportune time. But he didn't have the strength to protest. He just sucked in a deep breath, thankful to finally be home. That bitch Candace who played the role of good Samaritan, only to wind up teasing him to a raging hard-on before leaving him high, dry and on the side of the road, wouldn't figure into his explanation anyway.

"I'm…I'm sorry," was all Richard managed to get out.

"Yeah, you will be, my love. This was MY night out with my friends? How often does that happen?"

More than most wives, Richard thought, but didn't dare say. He'd learned to hold his tongue ever since Becky learned of his affair with their babysitter Amber's feet – and her ratty moccasins, the one's Amber had used to ensnare him in her duplicitous little game after he'd stupidly offered to buy them. That fateful night had been four years ago, and he'd paid time and again for his fetish-fueled indiscretion. Most precipitously when Becky and her friend Stephanie left him tied up and had Amber come work him over.

The little vixen, who was home from college at the time, had conspired with her best friend Lauren to drive him mad with lust. The evening was long and hard, and they'd watched laughing, nearly spitting out their Red Bull as he bucked his hips trying desperately for friction that would take him over the edge, a luxury he'd never get. At various times Amber and Lauren had planted either their shapely feet or the shoes they'd been wearing all day over his face, exasperating him in a way calculated to best rock the senses of the deplorable likes of him.

And Becky...he burned just thinking about it. She and Stephanie had gone wild themselves – with his credit card while he was helplessly tied down. While Amber and Lauren brought him to the brink over and over again, his wife and her friend were trying on clothes and designer shoes at the large mall downtown. No way would he have thought the handbags, sunglasses, heels, faux-leather skirts, blouses and panties they'd purchased would strain up against his credit limit, which he only learned when the bill arrived. Becky had virtually guffawed when she noticed him opening the envelope, his eyes bulging as surely as his dick was three weeks earlier.

Lesson learned. His incorrigible lust, combined with her new-found knowledge of his most secret sexual wants, had given her leverage in their relationship, and she wielded it frequently. If a gun was put to his head he'd be forced to admit that he wouldn't want to go back to the old way.

"What can I do?" he snarled, a bit more edge in his tone than he'd intended. "It wasn't a good night."

"Well, it's going to get worse...for you at least," she shot back.

"I'm not sure it can," Richard replied.

"Oh yes, it can."

As he dragged his body up the stairs, he heard her red nails tapping on her cell phone.

"Hi Joan. Listen, he just walked in...I know, he's useless. The kids are asleep. Why don't you, Kirsten, and Stephanie come over here for a little while. We'll have a nightcap...and I'll have a little demonstration for you!"

This last froze Richard near the top of the stairwell.

"Uh huh. Yes. No, don't be silly, it's not that late. And the bar here is stocked."

A pause, then Richard heard his wife say, "I see. So is Stephanie into this guy? Yeah? Then bring him along if that's what it takes to get her here!"

Richard didn't know what was going on, but he didn't like the sound of it. He was in no mood for company, especially the feminine kind.

"Yes. We'll be here," Becky said, turning her gaze toward her husband at the top of the stairs and smiling. "We'll see you soon. Oh, what are you ladies wearing tonight? Ah, perfect!"

She ended the call, then followed Richard up the stairs. "Where are you going?"

"I'm exhausted, gonna take a shower and lie down."

"Oh, OK, sweetie. But when you get out, don't put anything on. I'm still pissed and you're going to be held to account."

Four years his junior, Becky possessed an impish quality that made her appear even younger than her 42 years. There was an exuberance in everything she did, which is one of things that first attracted Richard to her. That and her long, muscular legs, wavy blond hair that seemed to require little maintenance, and a pretty face that turned downright sexy when she smirked or smiled with her perfect teeth. Her meticulous way with makeup, especially her choice of rich-hued lipstick, made her a downright head-turner.

All this made Richard's groin begin to stir at her admonishment. *What the hell's wrong with me, he thought. Why can't I reclaim some of my manhood when I'm in her presence? What happened with Amber was years ago. How is she still controlling me with it?* He could only conclude that a big, deeply seated part of him enjoyed her control.

"Yes," he mumbled.

"What's that?"

"I said yes." He turned toward the large bathroom.

Draped in only a towel 30 minutes later, hair still damp, Richard heard the doorbell. He peered down the stairs to see Kirsten, Joan, Stephanie, and a well-dressed 40-something man with slicked back hair and a two-day growth of whiskers enter. He didn't know what, exactly, the evening held in store, but he was nervous thinking about it. For now, he just sat disconsolately on the king-size bed, trying to be as quiet as he could. Maybe, just maybe, Becky would get involved with entertaining her friends and forget he was even in the house.

And as the minutes ticked by, Richard dared to believe that might be the case. He heard laughter and loud talking from the living room. Glasses newly filled with various spirits clinked. And a lot more laughing. The group was having a very good time, he surmised as he lay back on the bed, scrolling through his cell phone. He thought he might even fall asleep, his body weary from the long walk home.

"Sweetheart?" came the call as he began to doze. "Come down and say hello to my friends!"

No, he thought, they'd forgotten about him, hadn't they? He didn't move, or answer right away.

"Richard, come down now…and come as you are!"

Sensing the inevitable, he slowly got up, then with as much delay as he could muster descended the stairs, while securing the towel firmly around his waist.

"Here's the reason I couldn't meet you all at the restaurant," Becky said, by way of introduction. Then, to him, "come down, please, hurry up."

The ladies chuckled at his nearly naked body, but Kirsten's eyes widened too. Richard strove to keep fit, and her reaction, oddly enough, instilled him with a bit of pride.

For his part, Richard was taken aback by the three female guests. He'd met them all, and god knows Stephanie had seen much more of him than he'd care to remember, but they were all decked out in their man-killer finest. It was almost as though they were trying a bit too hard for women their age to look 10 years younger, to catch the roving eye, especially since Joan and Kirsten were married, but boy, did they look hot!

Joan, who had curly brown hair and was pushing 50, was rocking a white sleeveless cotton dress with barely-there nude hose and beige, three-inch peep-toe heels, a hint of dark red toenails peeking out. As Richard took in the view, she crossed her left leg over her right in a magnificent sweeping arch, then crossed her hands, weighed down with multiple rings, on her left thigh.

Kirsten, about his wife's age and thin, with a hint of freckles and pretty blond hair which she wore in a tight bun, wore a metallic, multi-color blouse and short black suede skirt. Her bare legs gleamed in the light atop patent black pumps.

And Stephanie, his wife's best friend who delighted in tormenting him that evening so long ago…she'd be ravishing in his mind if she wore a cloth sack. This night, however, she donned an intricately patterned black and gold linen dress that hugged her beautiful shape, complemented by deep burgundy, pointy-toe heels. Like Joan, she wore nude hose, but added a delicate anklet underneath on her right ankle. It was all he could do to keep his tongue inside his mouth as he watched her cross, then uncross, her legs. Her left hand, manicured with a shade nearly matching her pumps, crept up the thigh of the unidentified male.

"Hello," Richard muttered.

A chorus of hi's in return, then his wife said, "and this is Derek, Steph's new friend." Richard simply said "Hey," to which Derek amenably replied, "Hey, how's it going?" He was in his late 30s, a few years younger than his date.

"Sounds like you've been having fun," Richard then offered, hoping to keep the focus on them.

"We have, but it would've been nice to be out dancing," Becky said. "I told my friends they'd get a little demonstration of what happens when you defy me."

How the hell could I be held responsible for a car problem, he thought indignantly. Yet he knew Becky, and he especially knew she wouldn't abide any protestations from him, especially in front of her friends. "Yes," he croaked, his face reddening.

He took in his wife's lovely form as she moved to the club chair in the corner of the living room. She looked sexy in a black cotton dress that ended three inches above her knees, and accented with a thin silver belt and silver zipper up the back. She was bare-legged but wore the navy blue pumps he adored on her. Significant toe cleavage poked out of her shoes.

"Take down the towel please, Richard," she commanded.

Richard was startled. Except for that one night with Stephanie, she'd never displayed him in front of anyone. Was she serious?

"Um, Becky, I'd like – "

"Towel down," she snapped calmly, now pointing at the floor.

He scanned the room, noticing the anticipatory looks on his wife's guests' faces. His eyes shot up to the ceiling, buying time, or debating his options. He found none. There was nothing but a cotton towel between his dignity and his shame. Derek's presence sure didn't help.

"Eyes down, Richard. Look at my guests."

He sucked in a deep breath, momentarily frozen. He looked from one spectator to the next, their wide eyes goading him on. He felt an erection coming up, and was mortified that it would tent the towel.

"For heaven's sake, walk to me if you'd like," Becky said, offering him a shred of salvation.

Richard haltingly turned toward his wife, and as he took the four steps to where she was sitting unhooked the makeshift knot of the gray towel. It fell to the floor, and his ass was bared for all. Unbridled, his penis sprang up but it was mostly shielded from their view, for now.

"Across my legs, sweetie," his wife said softly, almost lovingly. Then to her friends, "we've planned this little demonstration for you. Hopefully, Dickey here will think twice before returning late again."

We? Richard bristled at the word. He breathed deeply, but remained standing for a moment, seeking a way out. She'd spanked him on occasion, but again, only in private. His forehead broke out in a sweat.

"Yes, I know, this is a new experience," Becky cooed, again reading his mind. "But I'm sure having an audience will make this quite scintillating, don't you think dear?"

He said nothing. He glanced over his shoulder, saw Stephanie now actively rubbing Derek's crotch. For his part, the only other male in the room turned his head and began kissing her deeply.

"Please…Becky, don't do this. I'm begging."

"Across my legs, Dickey," she repeated. She picked up her cell phone. "If you'd rather, I can call Amber." A broad but wicked grin erupted on her face. "I suspect she'd very much enjoy administering your punishment. Maybe she'll even wear her old moccasins for the occasion, hah!" Joan and Kirsten tittered, while Stephanie remained enraptured with Derek.

"No...no, not that," Richard stuttered, a new wave of shame coming over him at the mere mention of her name. Their former babysitter from years before certainly delighted in his abasement, as she'd proven a couple of times now. Nonetheless, the instant image his mind conjured of being bent over and spanked by Amber's pretty, delicate hand – in front of guests, no less – caused his dick to throb unbidden. Its girth increased.

"Oh my god!" Joan exclaimed, pointing at it and nudging Kirsten.

He remained still, as his wife hit Amber's name on her contact list and put the phone on speaker. On the second ring, he blurted, "No, hang up!"

"Then across my legs."

Defeated, he assumed a prone position over her smooth legs. Honestly, it was delightful to make contact with them, despite his humiliation. With a roughness that took him off guard, and that wasn't entirely necessary, Becky's hand grabbed his cock and maneuvered it between her sexy white thighs. She clamped them together. He was trapped, fully exposed, and helpless in front of three gorgeous women and one increasingly horny guy.

Becky glanced knowingly at her friends, then said "that's an extra 10 swats for defying me, dear. It's so much easier if you just comply the first time, isn't it?"

Richard could only gulp in anticipation of the terrible humiliation to come.

"Isn't it?"

"Yes, Becky, it is," he muttered.

The women chuckled, getting more and more excited about the spectacle unfolding before them. Richard heard them, but he was looking straight down at the floor. He didn't know Joan and Kirsten very well, but knew he could never bear to be in a room with either of them again. Stephanie had already stared into his pathetic soul and seen the depths of his depravity, and heard the tales from Becky.

"Good boy. Let's get to it, shall we?"

Before he could even think of how to respond, his wife's hand slammed into his ass with more force than he thought she could muster. He gasped, eyes remaining locked on the floor.

"Turn your head, dear, don't ignore our guests."

What? How could he? Somehow, he summoned the strength to look at their audience. Derek and Stephanie were really getting into each other now, and his hands were rubbing up under her dress.

SWAT! Richard whimpered, oddly noticing a bit of sympathy in the pretty eyes of the two women who were actually paying attention.

THWAP! The slaps continued. At one point he yelped loudly, to which his tormentress replied, "Shhh…it's OK, sweetheart, just 11 more to go."

Despite himself, his cock pulsed between his wife's satiny smooth thighs. Each blow caused him to piston downward, delivering more friction, and his mind fleetingly turned to the horrifying thought of possibly ejaculating in front of an audience. Through moistening eyes, he saw Stephanie and her new beau locking lips passionately, his hands now rubbing her breasts. But Richard dared not make eye contact with the others, lest he lose control of himself.

But Becky's legs were well-tuned into the physiology and suffering of her husband, and there was no way his throbbing could escape her notice, even as her spanking picked up momentum.

"Kirsten, do me a favor and take off your shoe," Becky said, the ever-polite hostess.

Slightly befuddled, the freckled beauty slipped off her right pump, her red-painted toes embracing their new-found liberation with a wiggle that drew Richard's pained gaze.

"Stand here," Becky said pointing, "right in front of him. Cup your heel over his face, please. Dickey, look forward!"

Another hard slap ensured compliance. Kirsten, in order to walk to them, had to remove her left pump. She now stood barefoot. Crouching down she placed the sloping insole of her right shoe against Richard's nose.

What did Becky tell her friend about me, Richard wondered in a frenzy, clenching his teeth against the assault on his rear but fully sucking in the aroma of Kirsten's teasing shoe. Did she also know about Amber? About the moccasins??

Around the shoe, all he could now see was Kirsten's smirk. If she didn't know about his fetishes before, she surely would now,

Richard thought, utterly humiliated. He groaned loudly, then cried out at the next swat, the shoe muffling his plaintive wail.

He'd lost count, but surely this ordeal would soon come to an end. While the pain and stinging of his by-now red ass were horrible, the scene he imagined he presented was much worse to his psyche. The black pump pressed against his face, as delightful as it was, did nothing to mitigate his shame. If anything, it exacerbated it. His penis jerked wildly with the next slap.

"Oh my god," cried Joan, pointing at him. "He's stringing!" She and Kirsten burst out laughing, and Richard felt whatever little dignity he had left completely abandon him. Even Stephanie and Derek paused from making out to take a look.

Richard couldn't actually feel the tangible manifestation of his excitement, but he was indeed very excited, and felt the turmoil inside from his lower abdomen on down. His wife's firm hand coming down on him, the incessant rubbing of his penis against her pretty thighs, Kirsten's petulant smirk, the vinegary odor from her high heel pump shooting into his brain and, yes, even the embarrassment of all this happening in front of a living room-full conspired to bring him to the brink. The fact there was another, clearly Alpha, male watching everything seared his soul.

"Is he?" Becky asked, his pre-cum shielded from her view. She actually winked at Stephanie as she added, "I bet Amber would get a kick out of this!"

With that she delivered what would be the final slap, and it was a good one. Richard's body recoiled again, but now his upper body too shuddered with humiliation and his cock twitched in paroxysms of pleasure. Sensing his imminent debasement, Kirsten swiftly moved her second hand to the shoe and pressed it more firmly over his nose, virtually sealing the tapered upper to his cheeks and creating a redolent chamber for him to suck in air from. All the while, she looked into his reddening eyes. She did, in fact, know what she was dealing with.

Richard emitted a loud grunt that was muffled by the nefarious pump, and with an overwhelming feeling of dread began spurting cum all over the hardwood floor under Becky's legs. While the release felt wonderful below his waste, his mind kept his pleasure at bay as it reeled from the degrading spectacle he presented. Nonetheless, his penis was in control, and what felt like a quart of semen shot, oozed and finally dribbled to the floor. He vaguely heard someone in the room say "look at that," and heard soft laughter, both feminine and masculine.

His rear afire, and still trapped by his domineering wife's thighs, all Richard could do was go limp, his face still ensconced in Kirsten's high heel.

"From now on, keep better track of the time," Becky cooed in his ear, amid more tittering. "Because next time you're late, I'll let your babysitter do the honors."

New Year's Grief

The dildo-style vibrator was humming on low, which is exactly how I wanted it. There'd be enough of a buzz to keep him excited, and possibly erect, but it wouldn't be nearly enough to actually get him off. For all intents and purposes, he was in arousal purgatory. And strapped to the bed frame naked, spread eagled, he was helpless to do anything about it.

I was extremely excited myself thinking about it, but to all external eyes I was the perfect party hostess.

Yes, party hostess. With my boyfriend Gray helplessly bound in the master bedroom suite, I was entertaining multiple friends – both my female posse and a few of their partners. It was, after all, New Year's Eve. What better excuse for a champagne-fueled soiree? "Oh, Gray is traveling on business sadly, and was held over in Green Bay when the winter storm rolled in," I'd told my guests, time and again. They understood – a lot of people got socked in by the snow – and in time a select few would understand the lie as well.

For now, it was a matter of greeting my guests as they arrived, keeping piping-hot hors d'oeuvres coming from the oven in the kitchen, making sure beverage glasses remained full, and counting down the last couple of hours until midnight, when we'd all burst into Auld Lang Syne, no doubt. For Gray, it would be a matter of keeping his wits about him, trying not to moan too loudly, and contemplating the horror if somebody should stumble into the upstairs bedroom.

I crossed one of my black-stockinged legs that Gray adored over the other, letting my Louboutin black pump with festive tourmalines slip off my heel, devising ways to ensure that what he dreaded the most right now would actually come to pass. It was all I could do to keep from getting wet. He knew I was mischievous sexually, and sometimes could be a cruel tormentress, but this was a level of evil neither of us knew I possessed until just a few hours earlier.

"Let's play," I'd said to him. "We'll ring out the old year in kinky fashion, and who knows what the new year will bring." I licked my lips as I said it, playfully stroking my long nails up his thigh, turning him to mush and making him very agreeable to anything I'd suggest. We'd done a few bondage scenes before, so it was no great leap that he'd consent to be worked over by me while tied up. But he was clueless about what lay ahead. That is, until the doorbell rang the first time.

His head jerked, shocked, and he was likely distraught that some interloper would be cutting our encounter short, after some prolonged teasing but well before his climax. Silly boy thought the little red dress, hose and heels I had put on earlier were for his eyes and his benefit only. His naiveté was hilarious to me.

"Oh good, my first guest is here!"

"What? What guest?"

"Relax, sweetie, you didn't think I'd be teasing you all night did you?" I replied. "I'm not that cruel. We're having something of a New Year's party. Oh, did I forget to tell you?"

"What the hell, Krista? Let me up, I mean finish me off, or – "

"Hold that thought, dear, while I go get the door."

Clara, drop-dead gorgeous with high cheekbones and raven-black hair, and her equally fine-looking boyfriend Dan were the first to arrive, and we had chatted animatedly and loudly in the foyer. They thoughtfully brought a bottle of merlot with them. I could only smile inwardly at what Gray must've been thinking at that moment, hearing multiple voices from just down the stairs, with his lovely cock standing tall and leaking, the bedroom door left wide open.

I invited them to hand me their coats; I hung his in the closet but carried hers up to the bedroom.

Now acutely aware of the wide open door, Gray had shot me the cutest look of fear and embarrassment, all he could do so as not to reveal his compromised presence.

I'd laid Clara's jacket on the plush chair in the corner of the room, then closed the door. He now spoke in the equivalent of a stage whisper.

"Untie me, honey, please untie me!"

"No, I don't think so, dear. You don't even like a lot of my friends. You won't be missing anything," I cooed.

Upon seeing the distress in his eyes, I'd leaned over and affixed the vibrator to the underside of his penis, covered both phalluses with one of my knee-high stockings, and tied the whole thing off with a velcro strap. Looking at him devilishly, I turned the sex toy to low. His eyes closed and he emitted a soft moan.

I gagged him with a strategically placed pair of tan pantyhose, and for the crowning touch, tied one of my worn panties blindfold-like around his head. The satiny pink fabric was just translucent enough to let his eyes perceive light, and maybe even shadows, but not to fully see anything.

"Now just relax for a couple of hours," I'd said, chuckling. "I'll try to check in on you. In the meantime, I'll leave you to…your own devices." I couldn't help laughing a little harder.

Sitting here, in the living room, surrounded by 14 guests including nine girlfriends, I mused that a well-teased cock, strapped to a merciless vibrator, would be desperate to come. At the same time, its owner was perpetually on edge of another kind. What does that do to a man, I wondered. His manhood straining to cum, his mind pondering the terror of discovery. Does that make one more excited, or cause one to become flaccid at the prospect of complete humiliation? And if his hardness flagged, would his little humming companion perk it right back up? It would be a fascinating conversation to have later. I took a sip of my wine, thinking about how much I'd enjoy it.

"Krista, is there another bathroom I could use to refresh my make-up? The powder room is in use." Alicia was standing next to me. She'd arrived alone, but was always up for a night out, with or without men. Naturally flirtatious and easy with a laugh, and sporting wavy dark brown hair and sharp brown eyes that just invited you in, she was popular in any crowd.

"Sure, Alicia. You can use the upstairs bathroom in the master bedroom suite," I said, savoring what I had just potentially set in motion. Her rear tightly encased in a black minidress and long legs atop three-inch glittery gold heels, Alicia ascended the stairs. The master bathroom was to the immediate right when you walked through the double bedroom door, and with the room dimly lit there was the chance she'd walk right in without noticing my helpless hubby. If he remained dead silent, that is.

Surely he'd hear her footsteps, the door opening. If she didn't see him right away, he'd hear the bathroom light click on, the clicking of her heels on the tile bathroom floor, the faucet running. Alicia was rather fastidious, and she'd spend a few minutes in front of the mirror. Gray's breathing would grow deeper as he steeled himself for discovery. How delightfully intense those moments would feel for him. Time would slow.

Moving to the chair near the bottom of the stairs, my ears perked up for any sounds. The Pandora stream coming through the entertainment system would mask any reaction from my other guests, but I was tuned in.

A few minutes later, Alicia came back down, seemingly nonplussed. We exchanged a few words before she headed to the bar to get a fresh drink. Gray, it appeared, had caught a reprieve…for the moment.

A half hour went by, and my best friend Julie and her husband Matt moved toward the front door. Julie, blond, 32, with a well-toned body and movie-star white teeth, was the adventurous sort, and had shared some of her bedroom exploits with me over the years, as I'd done with her. Matt, it seemed, was quite the leg man, and I enjoyed her stories of how she liked to tease him with her beautiful stems, often encased in her trademark patterned hosiery. Every now and then, she'd let her husband fuck her legs like a dog in heat, and if he'd done something to annoy her she'd simply separate her legs at the moment of climax. Tonight she wore polka dot hosiery beneath a green velvet dress, with matching suede green 4-inch heels. Poor Matt couldn't decide whether to look at her legs or mine, as I sat with one leg bent and tucked under the other.

"It was a wonderful party, but we have to go before midnight, I'm afraid. Our sitter has plans later," Julie said apologetically.

"Oh, I understand completely. Your coat is upstairs on the bedroom chair. I'm so glad you two could make it."

Julie headed up the stairs; Matt, looking very fuck-able in black pants, white button-front shirt and a sport coat, continued studying my lower half while trying to keep up pleasant conversation. I'm certain he thought about doing the same to my legs as he'd done with his wife's. I wondered if I would be as mean as her. I let my left shoe fall off my toes as I thought about what was inevitably going to happen upstairs. My panties were wet.

Once again, my senses were on high alert, and this time I was rewarded with a high-pitched gasp, barely noticeable over Katie Perry coming from the speakers. Gray had been seen. I tried without much success to mentally put myself in his position. He had no vision, so he wouldn't know just who had entered the room unless Julie decided to talk to him. Helpless and surely throbbing, Gray would be turning 50 shades of red upon hearing the shock of a female intruder. Not being able to see would be a blessing to him at that moment, as he'd be too ashamed to make eye contact anyway. Would he be struggling at his binding? Beseeching his observer through the gag for help, or for some form of understanding?

What a mind-fuck, I thought. He'd never know for sure who it was in the room with him, and so he'd feel humiliated every time he saw any of my friends from here on. It was delicious.

I reached for my cell phone, pretending to listen to whatever Matt was saying about New Year's resolutions, and swiped to the app that controlled the vibrator via Bluetooth. After a few seconds of deliberation – I could really be an evil bitch when I wanted to – I ran my fingertip over the slider that controlled speed, increasing it from a frustrating but low-impact 3 to a scintillating but not quite ejaculation-inducing 6. There'd be more to come, perhaps, but the night was still young.

After an exceedingly long time to simply retrieve a coat – Matt hadn't noticed, still transfixed by my leg show – Julie bounced back down the stairs, a big grin on her face. Her eyes caught mine and I read a combination of girlish mischief and admiration there.

"Happy New Year, Krista!" she sang as they walked out the door. "I'm sure you will have a very fun start to the new year!"

Gray would be reticent to talk in detail about what had transpired, because of his utter humiliation at it all. But I knew I could count on Julie to share what happened. After all, isn't that what BFFs are for? And she didn't disappoint.

Upon walking in the room, she said later, she first noticed a slight buzzing sound, and when she turned to the source she found my husband buck naked, arms and legs stretched out, his cock sticking straight up. As she walked closer, she saw the vibrator, inside of my black stocking, but it had fallen askew. She sat down on the bed, at which point my hubby's head turned to the side, as if trying to bury itself in the pillow.

He whimpered quietly, so she shushed him in a soft, motherly tone. Believing he was badly trying to cum, but seeing the poor thing had lost most contact with the vibrator, she took pity on him. She removed the stocking and was going to simply set the vibrator back in place, but the veiny, rock hard penis was just too appealing, she said. It was almost purple and seemed to be beckoning to be teased. Throwing caution to the wind, she gave it five firm but very slow strokes. Gray's whimpers turned to guttural moans. Then she held the toy flush against the underside of his cock, pulled the knee-hi tight back over it, and re-fastened the Velcro strap. She stood up and began to walk out, but said a devilish idea struck her when she passed my closet.

Julie noticed one of my beige patent pumps and picked it up. She took a quick whiff, concluding that it had been well worn, then turned off the bedroom light. She returned to my helplessly bound husband and maneuvered the pump over his face, with the heel cup wedged under the gag and the pointed toe resting beneath my panties, over his eyes. She tightened both the gag and the blindfold and, pleased with her work, stood up to leave. But she cocked her head back as she walked away from the bed, noticing the hum get louder. It happened that it was at precisely that moment I increased the vibrator speed. His moaning was music to her ears, she said.

And Julie's tale would be music to my own. But for this evening, I could only picture what poor Gray was going through in my mind's eye.

When midnight rolled around, we did in fact sing Auld Lang Syne with vigor, loud enough that he would hear our rendition from the bedroom and know that the party would imminently be breaking up. I had strategically collected the women's coats in the bedroom, while hanging the few men's jackets in the coat closet.

"Your coats are too pretty to squeeze in there, and there aren't enough free hangars anyway," I'd told them during the evening.

Of course, Gray could only estimate how many coats I'd brought into the room. His sexual frustration had him too far gone, his senses too diminished, to keep any real tabs on my comings and goings. But I knew, and I'm sure he instinctively knew, that one garment was one too many in his compromised state. Nor could he know there weren't any men's coats among them, ratcheting up his distress even further. His predicament turned me on to no end!

My guests gradually began to leave. This would be the most difficult time for my husband. His embarrassment would be overwhelming, and surely he was far past thinking this would be fun. No, there'd be no enjoyment for him, only paralyzing fear. Even the buzzing vibrator wouldn't mitigate the turmoil going through his mind.

There was Clara, of course, wearing a tiny burgundy dress, and bare-legged despite the cold outside. There was Gretchen, my read-haired, cutely freckled former roommate, wearing an ugly Christmas sweater with reindeers humping, short blue skirt, tan pantyhose and blue suede ankle boots. Ness had arrived with her latest potential suitor, dressed to kill or maybe for some post-celebration action in a black cotton dress with wide silver belt, sheer black hose and festive black mesh-lace pumps.

Courtney, 41 and divorced, was my frequent partner in crime. Like Gretchen, she came alone but was always concerned with her appearance and open to a spontaneous encounter with the right guy. Tonight she wore a dark gray dress that ended well above her knees, taupe nylons that highlighted her gorgeous legs, and gray five-inch heels. And there was Jasmine, the 22-year-old who frequently cut my hair, a slightly heavy emo girl with bright red lipstick and horn-rimmed black glasses, and clad in a purple hoodie, opaque black tights, and thick-tread combat boots. Julie made a return trip to get her coat too. All had been imbibing, and those who'd indulged the most had already summoned Ubers.

One by one they and the others ascended the stairs to retrieve their coats. I heard occasional high-pitched shrieks, and knew I'd have some explaining to do, likely over drinks, in the next couple of days. Possibly, one or two would disapprove, but we'd eventually laugh it off together. As Courtney teetered back down the stairs, laughing uncontrollably and with eyes like saucers, I took a big sip of merlot, again opened the app on my phone, and slid the speed control up to its maximum setting.

About the Author

Gray Fisher has been writing erotica since 2007. Since then, he has published multiple stories in *Leg Show Magazine* and at www.bestlegshow.com. His first three fiction anthologies, ***The Playful Babysitter and Other Tales of Male Submission, Fetishism and Erotic Humiliation***, ***Trapped in Her Nylon Web and Other Tales of Fetishism and Erotic Humiliation***, and *Women, Wine and Heels and Other Tales of Fetishism and Erotic Humiliation*, are available in e-book and paperback at Amazon.

Follow Gray Fisher on Facebook at www.facebook.com/gray.fisher.376, and on Twitter, @fetishscribe.

www.ingramcontent.com/pod-product-compliance
Lightning Source LLC
Chambersburg PA
CBHW071446150726
48000CB00006B/2466